Best
School Year Yet

Megan Hoffman, MOTR/L

TULSA

ISBN: 978-1-954095-98-4

Best School Year Yet

Copyright © 2021 by Megan Hoffman, MOTR/L
All rights reserved.

No part of this publication may be reproduced, distributed, or transmitted in any form or by any means, including photocopying, recording, or other electronic or mechanical methods, without the prior written permission of the publisher, except in the case of brief quotations embodied in critical reviews and certain other noncommercial uses permitted by copyright law.

For permission requests, write to the publisher at the address below.

Yorkshire Publishing
1425 E 41st Pl
Tulsa, OK 74105
www.YorkshirePublishing.com
918.394.2665

Published in the USA

For Anna, Ryan, Martha Rose, Graham, Hank, Juliet, Mae, and my dearest Henry. You gave me hope during these uncertain times and joy on even the darkest days.

I woke up early one morning. It
was the first day of school!
I grabbed my new backpack—isn't it cool?

I brushed all my teeth and ran
a comb through my hair.
Flew down the stairs...I can't wait to get there!

In the kitchen, Mom and Dad both took a seat.
Pancakes for breakfast? Yum, what a treat!

As I slurped down my OJ and gobbled my eggs,
Mom started to speak while
Dad nodded his head.

They said that some things will
be different this year,
and I smiled real big as it all became clear.

"We got you this mask to wear
with your friends."
They paused: "This might be where
your questions begin?"

My mind, it was swirling as my
words all poured out.
I got so excited that I started to shout!

A mask like a hero, soaring high in the skies,
bravely defending and saving our lives!

Or a mask like the costumes we
wear on Halloween night,
tricking and treating in a fun, frenzied fright.

Or a mask like an actor up on a stage?
Lights, camera, action! The crowd below raves.

My parents grinned and continued,
all matter-of-fact:
"Well, yes, honey, and there's
more to it than that."

"To stay safe and healthy, keep
arms' distance from others."
And that's where I stopped them
and started to wonder...

Distance apart? A magical force
field, protecting with might?
Warding off germies, sickness and plight!

Or distance for dancing? I
take a twirl and a bow.
In the spotlight, I'm singing: I can picture it now!

Or distance for running, leaping
and skipping about?
I have room now to dash, dart
and jump up and down!

My parents grinned and
continued matter-of-fact:
"Well, honey, there's still more to it than that."

"You must wash your hands
and clean off your toys,
so you don't spread germs to
other girls and boys."

Washing and cleaning? Like a car
wash with bubbles and lights?
Sudsy splishes and splashes
from morning to night!

Washing and cleaning like waves
that crash onto the beach?
Water swirling and whirling away
sand from my feet?

Or washing and cleaning like a water gun war?
Squirting, soaking and laughing
'til my tummy is sore!

"I think I'm getting it now.
Thanks, Mom and Dad!
I can follow these rules, they sound super rad."

They giggled and hugged me. "Yes, you sure are!
Now one last thing to remember
for our little star..."

"If a classmate gets sick, then
you must stay home.
School will still happen on a screen or a phone."

Stay home like a snow day any time of the year,
playing outside without my snow gear?

Stay home like a holiday, all merry and bright?
With family and friends still near and in sight!

Or at home like a sick day with
warm noodle soup?
Home means cuddles and PJs
and all my toys too!

"That's it!" they exclaimed.
"You've it got, sweet child.
We're happy to see you still share our smile!"

I winked, cleared the table and
washed both my hands.
Look at me practicing this new list of demands!

Mom and Dad beamed as they took in the sight.
I must have surprised them with
my try and my might!

I gave them a hug and said not to fret.
From the sound of it, this could be
our best school year yet!